To Alison, with much love
Viv

For Martha and Sophie, with love
Chris

First published 1994 by
Walker Books Ltd, 87 Vauxhall Walk
London SE11 5HJ

This edition published 1999

2 4 6 8 10 9 7 5 3

Text © 1994 Vivian French
Illustrations © 1994 Chris Fisher

This book has been typeset in Monotype Perpetua.

Printed in Hong Kong

British Library Cataloguing in Publication Data
A catalogue record for this book is
available from the British Library.

ISBN 0-7445-6941-9

PLEASE,
PRINCESS PRIMROSE!

WRITTEN BY
VIVIAN FRENCH

ILLUSTRATED BY
CHRIS FISHER

WALKER BOOKS
AND SUBSIDIARIES
LONDON · BOSTON · SYDNEY

PRINCESS PRIMROSE
woke up early
on her birthday
and marched downstairs.

"Where are my presents?" she demanded as she sat down at the breakfast table.

"Shut your eyes, my tiddly umpty birthday poppet," said the Queen.

"No peeping!" said the King. The Cook came in with a pile of presents.

The Cook's boy came behind her, carrying the teapot.

"NOW!" they all said.
Princess Primrose
opened her eyes.
"Happy birthday,
my darling sweetest
pudding," said the Queen.
"Oh," said Primrose,
and she tore the paper
off her presents.

"A teddy bear
and a train set. HUH!
I wanted a gold coach
with six white horses."

"Happy birthday,
my itsy bitsy princess,"
said the King.
"What's this?" said
Primrose, ripping
open another parcel.
"BAH! A skipping rope.
I wanted my very own
magician with a blue cloak
with silver stars on it."

"Happy birthday,
Princess Primrose,"
said the Cook.
"YUCK!" said Primrose.
"A cookery book. I
wanted a magic mirror."

The Cook's boy stared at Primrose.
"Isn't she rude?" he whispered.
"Sssh, dear," said the Cook.

"Where's my cake?" demanded Primrose. "I want to blow out my candles."

"Birthday tea at four o'clock, my teeny angel pussycat," said the Queen.

"HUMPH!" said Primrose. "So what are we going to do all day?"

"Er…" said the Queen. "Ar…" said the King. "I'm just off to make the cake," said the Cook, and she hurried out.

The Cook's boy tugged at the Queen's arm. "Why don't we play a game?"
Primrose sat up. "What did you say?"

"Why don't we play a game?" said the Cook's boy. "What about hide-and-seek?"
"I don't know how," said Primrose.

"I'll show you," said the Cook's boy. "You can hide, and I'll find you."

The Cook's boy
shut his eyes and
counted to ten while
the King and the Queen
and Primrose hid
in the attic.
"Coming! Ready
or not!" shouted
the Cook's boy.

The King shut his eyes
and counted to ten while
the Queen and Primrose
and the Cook's boy
hid in the bedroom.
"Whoopee! Here I come!"
shouted the King.

The Queen shut her
eyes and counted to ten
while Primrose and the
Cook's boy and the King
hid in the bathroom.
"Coooeee!
I'm on my way!"
called the Queen.

Primrose shut her eyes and counted to ten while the Cook's boy and the King and the Queen hid in the kitchen.

"One two three – it's ME!" she shouted, and she found the Cook's boy and the King and the Queen in no time at all.

"Four o'clock!" said the Cook, coming in with the cake.
"Time for a lovely tea for my bestest poppety parcel," said the Queen, puffing hard.

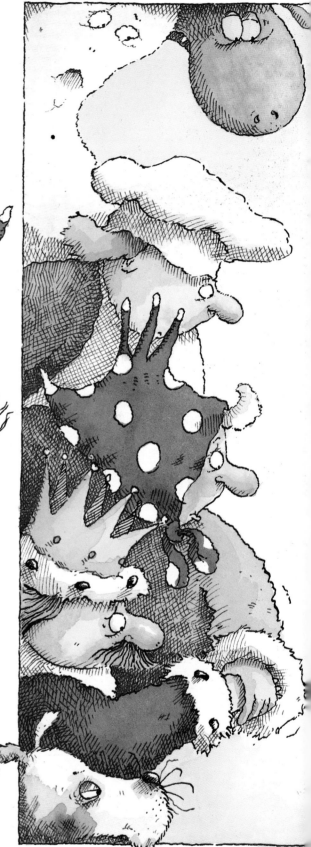

"Bother," said Primrose. "I want to go on playing." She looked at the Cook's boy.
"You can play with me after tea," she said. "And tomorrow. And

the next day."
"No," said the Cook's boy.

"I don't want to. Well – not unless you ask nicely."

The King and the Queen and the
Cook stared at him. Then they looked
at Primrose and held their breath.
Princess Primrose made a strange
noise. The King and the Queen held
hands tightly. The noise grew louder,
and the Cook edged nearer to the door.

"P... P... PLEASE!"

"P...P...P...PLEASE!"
said Princess Primrose.
"PLEASE will you
play with me?"

The Cook's boy bowed.
"Of course, Princess,"
he said. "It'll be fun."

P. . .

"Can we play too?" asked
the King and the Queen.
Primrose put her head on
one side. "Maybe," she said.
"If you ask nicely."

"Oh," said the King and
the Queen. "Please?"
Princess Primrose curtsied.
"Of course," she said. "And
now I want you all to sing
Happy Birthday to me."

"Well…" said the Cook's boy.

"PLEASE!" said Princess Primrose.

"It'll be a pleasure," said the Cook's boy and the Cook and the Queen and the King. And they did.

MORE WALKER PAPERBACKS
For You to Enjoy

Some more picture books by Vivian French

A SONG FOR LITTLE TOAD
Illustrated by Barbara Firth

Everyone has got different advice for Mother Toad as she tries to sing her baby to sleep.
But there's only one song that Little Toad really wants to hear in this enchanting story,
which was shortlisted for the Smarties Book Prize.

"A good story to read aloud. Barbara Firth's toads are the most
expressive outside *Wind in the Willows*." *Child Education*

0-7445-5299-0   £4.99

LAZY JACK
Illustrated by Russell Ayto

Jack's so lazy he never opens his eyes from morning till night.
Every day he does a different job and every evening he makes a terrible mess of
bringing back his wages. You just can't help but laugh at his crazy antics
in this modern retelling of a favourite tale.

0-7445-4721-0   £4.99

ONCE UPON A TIME
Illustrated by John Prater

A little boy tells of his "dull" day, while all around a host of
favourite nursery characters act out their stories.

"The pictures are excellent, the telegraphic text perfect, the idea brilliant.
We have here a classic, I'm sure, with an author-reader
bond as strong as *Rosie's Walk*." *Books for Keeps*

0-7445-3690-1   £4.99